Moby Pincher's Hurricane Adventure

By
Dee Scallan

Illustrated by 9-year old
Daniel Myers

Bookman LLC
Publishing & Marketing

Providing Quality, Professional
Author Services

www.bookmanmarketing.com

ISBN: 1-59453-720-8

DEDICATION

I would like to dedicate this book to my wonderful, loving parents: Earnest M. Martin and Verna Vee Martin who taught me to believe in myself, and to reach for the moon, knowing that if I should miss, I will surely land on a star.

Moby Pincher was born deep in the beautiful green swamplands of south Louisiana. Moby was different from the other crawbabies because he was so-o-o big and he had very, very large pinchers.

1

As the years passed, Moby grew larger and larger until he was twice as big as the other crawfish. His huge size caused the crawfish in his town to fear him. They would not talk to Moby, or let him play in any crawfish games, not even crawball.

   One day as Moby, with great big crawfish tears in his eyes, was
sitting on an old cypress tree stump, his friend Tu Tu turtle came by.
"Why are you crying, Moby?" asked Tu Tu. "I don't have any
crawfish friends because they think I will hurt them. If only I could
prove to them that I'm a good kind hearted crawfish," said Moby.
"Don't worry, Moby," replied Tu Tu. "One day they will realize how
nice and kind you are and you'll have lots and lots of friends." Moby
told Tu Tu goodbye and sadly started crawling home. As he crawled
through the swamp, it started to rain a slow, steady drizzle.

Moby hurried to crawl down into his mudhole where it was dry a warm.

As the rain lulled Moby to sleep, he began to dream about all the crawfish friends he would like to have.

Outside, the cold raindrops came down harder and harder, and the wind blew stronger and stronger bending the moss covered tree down to the ground. A bad storm called a hurricane was moving in across Lake Pontchatrain towards the swamplands.

As the wind rose higher and the rain came down harder, the muddy water in the bayou started to rise higher and higher. The water rose so fast, so quick that it started washing the crawfish out of their mudhouses all along the bayou.

Suddenly, Moby was awakened by a loud knock on his door. "Wake up, Moby, " yelled Tu Tu . "You've got to save Crawfish Town!"

Moby hurried out of his hole and followed Tu Tu through the pouring rain until they came to the old pirogue boat that had been left abandoned on the side of the bayou.

Moby took his giant pinchers and pushed the pirogue boat, with Tu Tu inside, until it slipped off the bank into the water.

It took all the strength Moby had to push the pirogue boat
through the water with the wind blowing against him and the rain
hitting him so hard in the face. Moby could barely see through the
blinding rain as the crawfish swam toward the pirogue boat and
Tu Tu pulled each safely into the old boat.

Finally, after every crawfish was safely in the pirogue boat, the rain and wind slacked. Moby saw a high spot on the bayou bank and with all his might he gave one last big shove and pushed the pirogue boat on the bank.

As the eye of the storm passed over Crawfish Town, the wind and rain came to a stop. The heavy warm air became still and it was eerily silent. But Moby and his friends were not fooled by the sudden change in the weather. They knew the hard driving rain and the strong blowing wind would soon hit the swamp again, but from the opposite direction. They quickly dug holes in dark brown soil and crawled into the holes pulling the dirt in after them.

Moby's friends knew from instinct when it was safe to dig out of their holes. As they carefully looked out, they were happily surprised to see a beautiful rainbow shining through the misty rain.

When the rain stopped and the water in the bayou drained, the crawfish started to clean up their mudhouses.

Moby crawled back to his mudhouse very tired but very happy because he had helped save the crawfish.

On the next day Moby found a letter in his mailbox. It was from the crawfish inviting him to a party on the bank of the bayou. This made Moby very happy.

Moby could see the crawfish gathering for the party. They were eating rice burgers and dancing to Cajun music.

   Once Moby reached the party, all the crawfish came running over
to him thanking him for saving them from the hurricane. If it had
not been for Moby, they would have been washed away never to see
their homes again. Moby was a hero.

Moby smiled and danced with joy, and all the happy crawfish circled around him singing proudly "For he's a Jolly good Crawfish." But Moby was the happiest crawfish of all because his dream had come true – he had lots and lots of friends.

Hurricane Facts

Hurricanes gather heat & energy though contact with ocean water. Evaporation from the seawater increases their power. The combination of heat and moisture along with the right wind conditions can create a hurricane. Hurricanes are powerful storms that measure several hundred miles in diameter. They have 2 main parts. The first is the eye of the hurricane, which is a calm area in the center of the storm. Usually the eye of a hurricane measures about 20 miles in diameter and has very few clouds. The second part is the wall of clouds that surrounds the calm eye. This is where the hurricane's strongest winds and heaviest rain occurs. Hurricanes rotate in a counter-clockwise direction around the "eye". They have winds at least 74 miles per hour. When they come onto land, the heavy rain, strong winds & heavy waves can damage buildings, cars, and trees. The heavy waves are called a storm surge. Storm surges are very dangerous and a major reason why you must stay away from the ocean during a hurricane warning or a hurricane.

Hurricanes are classified into five categories based on their wind speeds and potential to cause damage. They are as follows:

CATEGORY

One-   winds 75-95- miles per hour
Two-   winds 96-110 miles per hour
Three- winds 111-130 miles per hour
Four-   winds 131-155 miles per hour
Five-   winds greater than 155 miles per hour

Important terms to know:

Hurricane Watch- means a hurricane is possible within 36 hours. Stay tuned to the radio and television for more information.
Hurricane Warning- A hurricane is expected within 24 hours. You may have to evacuate and make plans for pets.

Hurricane season occurs from June 1st to November 30th, but they can happen any time of the year.

Hurricanes are named by the National Weather Service. Some of the largest and well known hurricanes are as followed:

- Hurricane Carla (September 10, 1961) hit Texas coast, winds were 150 miles per hour $2 billion in damage.

- Hurricane Betsy (September 8, 1965) hit Florida and then turned and hit Louisiana; winds were 160 miles per hour. Third most costly hurricane in the U.S. $6.5 billion in damage.

- Hurricane Camille (August 13, 1969) Category 5 hurricane the most powerful rating winds were as high as 200 miles per hour. It hit the Gulf Coast but caused flooding in Virginia. Fifth most costly at $5.2 billion.

- Hurricane Celia (August 3, 1970) Hit Texas- $1.6 billion in damage.

- Hurricane Gilbert (September 16, 1988)

  Category 5 winds 160 miles per hour. Hit Jamaica, then Mexico, and came to the U.S. (Texas & Oklahoma) as heavy rain storms.

- Hurricane Andrew (August 24, 1992)

  Hit Southern Florida, then turned and hit Louisiana. Heavy rains and tornados were part of hurricanes. Most expensive hurricane in U.S. history.

- Hurricane Floyd (September 1999)

  North Carolina was hit the hardest. It brought so much rain that 13 states were issued disaster declarations. $500 million of federal money was spent helping states recover.

LOUISIANA WETLANDS

Moby says, "Please help save our Louisiana Wetlands." Louisiana is losing 25 to 35 square miles per year due to many factors, one being hurricane damage. In 2002, two hurricanes hit the Louisiana Coast within a two week period, in which tens of thousands of acres of already declining wetlands were torn up leaving water where there were once protective marshes. Louisiana was very fortunate that these category 4 hurricanes weakened before hitting Louisiana. Even as weakened storms they caused $700 million dollars of damage. The wetlands and barrier islands help protect Louisiana towns from hurricanes. What would happen if Louisiana is hit by a category 4 hurricane and we do not have the wetlands to provide protection?

Without the coastal wetlands protection, the storm surge will go further inland and what will happen to cities like New Orleans that are already below sea level? The loss of our Coastal Wetlands also puts the Louisiana Seafood industry in grave danger. This loss affects the entire nation. Without Louisiana's Coastal Wetlands what would happen to the migratory birds that rest and eat along the flight path. Moby is very concerned about our wetland crisis, but there are solutions that can save the wetlands so Moby says, "JUMP BACK and protect our wetlands."

We are hidden in the book.
Can you find us?

T – Bo Bumblebee

Cuz Caterpillar

Lu Lu Ladybug

Spencer Spider

How to draw Moby Pincher

1. Start by drawing the snout. Sketch a side-ways hershey's kiss to the right and then add a small curved line for the jaw.

2. Draw two skinny half eggs for the eyes. Add a curved line for the eyeballs.

Great job! Keep it up!

3. Add a curved line above each eye. Start at the tip of Moby's snout and draw a curved line to the left.

4. Draw two pointed bananas to the left behind the eyes. Add curved lines to finish Moby's antennas.

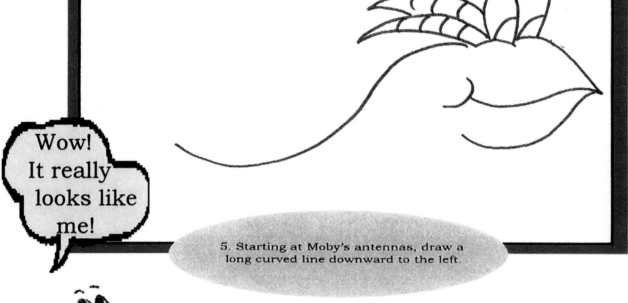

Wow! It really looks like me!

5. Starting at Moby's antennas, draw a long curved line downward to the left.

6. Add the pinchers by drawing two leaf shapes to the right at the bottom of Moby's snout. Add a zig-zag line in the middle of each leaf.

7. Add Moby's tail by drawing a three leaf clover to the left. Add two lines to the clover to finish Moby's tail.

8. Add three claws to the left. Add four lines along his back for detail. Now you have drawn Moby Pincher, the biggest most kind hearted crawfish in the South!

Terrific! He could pass for my twin!

About the Author

Dee Scallan was raised in Central Louisiana around Alexandria. She has lived in various cities in the state, including Baton Rouge, New Iberia and Lafayette. Mrs. Scallan is currently residing in West Monroe, Louisiana.

Dee has owned and operated a private pre-school for twenty-five years. She is affectionately known as "Miss Dee" to all of her students. Miss Dee created Moby Pincher stories for the storytime hour at her school, and the children loved them. Miss Dee continued to create the stories because the children would plead to hear them. Most of the stories center around a holiday. In the stories, Miss Dee attempts to familiarize the children with events, animals, insects, plants and other things that are native to Louisiana.

After the parents of the children started asking for copies of the Moby Pincher stories to read at home, Ms. Dee decided to publish them. It is Miss Dee's hope that children will be entertained by Moby's antics, while learning about the unique culture of the bayou land of Louisiana.

About the Illustrator

Daniel Myers is a nine-year-old boy who resides in West Monroe, Louisiana. Daniel demonstrated an artistic aptitude at the age of three years. Daniel is a former student of Ms. Dee's Montessori Preschool and is now in the third grade at Claiborne Elementary School. Daniel is active in the sport of soccer. He is the son of Ronnie and Tammy Myers of West Monroe, Louisiana.